Food +
Farming

For Hogan and Tamara

Copyright © 1999 by Ken Brown
The rights of Ken Brown to be identified as the author and illustrator of this work
have been asserted by him in accordance with the Copyright, Designs and Patents Act, 1988.
First published in Great Britain in 1999 by Andersen Press Ltd., 20 Vauxhall Bridge Road,
London SW1V 2SA. Published in Australia by Random House Australia Pty.,
20 Alfred Street, Milsons Point, Sydney, NSW 2061. All rights reserved.
Colour separated in Switzerland by Photolitho AG, Zürich.
Printed and bound in Italy by Grafiche AZ, Verona.

10   9   8   7   6   5   4   3   2

British Library Cataloguing in Publication Data available.

ISBN 0 86264 897 1

This book has been printed on acid-free paper

Lucky Mucky Pup

Written and illustrated by
Ken Brown

Andersen Press
London

Mucky Pup was snoozing in the sun
when a bee buzzed by.

He snapped at it.

He jumped at it.

crash

He pounced at it.

smash

But the bee buzzed on . . .

So Mucky Pup chased it –
into the vegetable garden . . .

WHOOPS

bzzz

and into the farmyard.

"Come on, Pig!" he called.
"Come and chase this bee with me!"

bzzz

SPLIIISH SPLOOOSH

They chased it through the barn . . .

cluck!

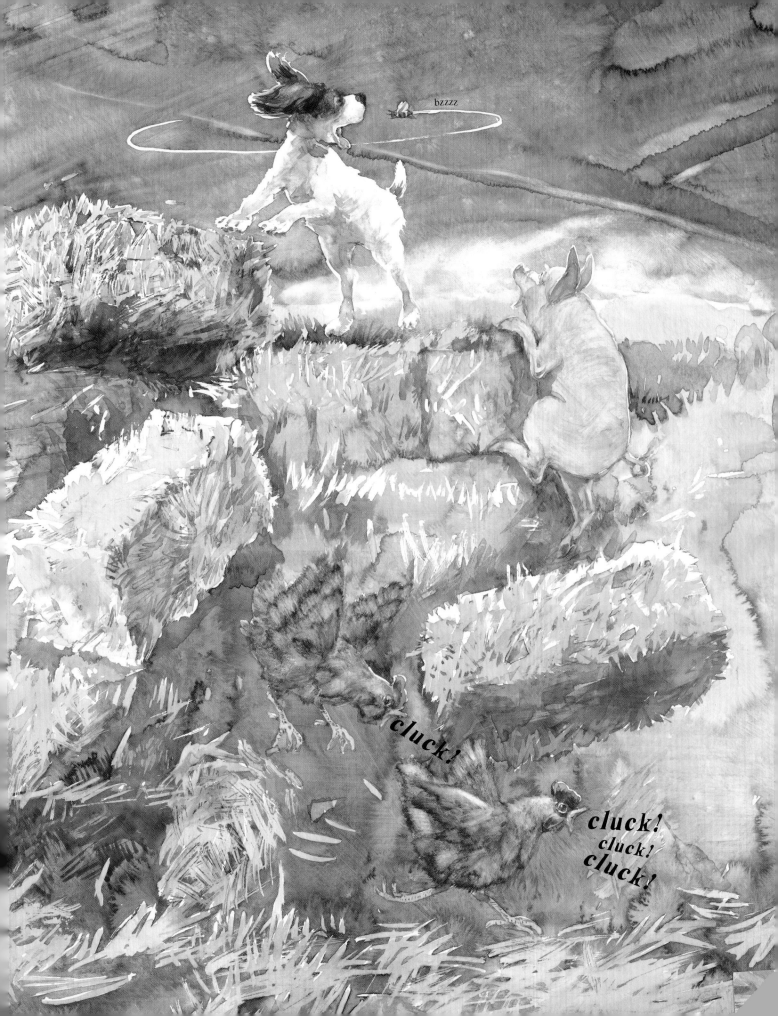

past the shed and around the pond

and into the meadow.

bbbbzzzzzbbbzbbbbbZzzbbbzzzzzzzzzz

"Where's that bee gone now?"
panted Mucky Pup.
"To fetch his friends," gasped Pig. "Look!"
Mucky Pup looked and . . . Uh-oh!

And how they ran! Out of the meadow . . .

past the shed and across
the pond . . .

back to the barn

and under the hay,

down the hill and into . . .

SPLAT!

. . . the farmyard,

into the garden and under the washing,
safe and sound!
    But . . .

"Mucky Pup! What have you been doing?"
wailed the farmer's wife.

"Poor Mucky Pup. *He's* not to blame," cried the children.
"He was being chased by that swarm of bees."

"Well, he's lucky they didn't catch him," said their mum.
"Come on, Mucky Pup,
let's clean you up."

So, instead of getting a scolding, Mucky Pup had a bath under the garden hose. And that was *much* more fun.
Lucky Mucky Pup!

Wuff!
Wuff!